SCRAPS OF TIME

A Song for Harlem

1928

by

PATRICIA C. MCKISSACK

illustrated by

GORDON C. JAMES

PUFFIN BOOKS

To Elise Csapo—P. C. McK.

*To my father Thomas, Uncle Gene, and
'Uncle' Andrew, three of Harlem's finest. —G. C. J.*

PUFFIN BOOKS
An imprint of Penguin Random House LLC
375 Hudson Street
New York, New York 10014

First published in the United States of America by Viking,
a division of Penguin Young Readers Group, 2007
Published by Puffin Books, a division of Penguin Young Readers Group, 2008

LIBRARY OF CONGRESS CATALOGING-IN-PUBLICATION DATA IS AVAILABLE.
ISBN 978-0-670-06209-6 (hc)

Puffin Books ISBN 9780142412381

Printed in the United States of America
Book design by Nancy Brennan

11 13 15 17 19 20 18 16 14 12

Contents

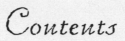

In Gee's Attic

"What are you looking for?" Trey asked his cousin Mattie Rae. Then he sneezed. The dust in the attic always made him sneeze.

"I'm looking for that magazine, the one I saw last time." Mattie Rae turned to her grandmother. "Gee, you said a poem in it was written by one of our relatives."

Gee took a copy of an old *Crisis* magazine from one of the trunks. She turned to page twelve. "Here it is," said Gee. "'A Song for Harlem.' It was written by Lilly Belle Turner."

"Who was she?" Trey asked. "Why did she write the poem? Where was she when she wrote it? What—?"

Gee laughed. "Wait a minute," she said, holding up her hands. "Lilly Belle was my aunt. She spent the summer of 1928 in New York as part of a young authors' writing project.

"Let me start from the beginning." Gee took an old notebook from the same trunk. "Aunt Lilly Belle always kept journals. Since she never married or had children, they all came to me when she passed away. So I think I know her story very well."

The three children gathered around their grandmother as she began the story of Lilly Belle Turner.

Chapter 1

In New York

Lilly Belle had woken up at first light. That's when she liked to write in her journal. It lay open in front of her on Aunt Odessa's kitchen table. But it was difficult to concentrate. Even though it was early Sunday morning, a day of rest, it was as noisy as a workday. In Harlem it was always like that. Didn't New Yorkers ever sleep?

Someone had played a saxophone until dawn. The bells on the streetcars clanged every few minutes. And the people across the hall had had an all-night party.

Lilly Belle closed her eyes and imagined being back home in Smyrna, Tennessee, on Sunday mornings: M'Dear stirring a pot at the kitchen stove and humming; her little brothers, James and Peter, scraping every bit of oatmeal with cinnamon out of their bowls; her father slurping hot coffee from his favorite tin cup. Oh, those good smells!

A car horn blasted and broke the magic of the moment. Lilly Belle opened her eyes. In Aunt Odessa's kitchen nothing was bubbling in a pot. And in the icebox there was only a bunch of carrots, a bowl of something disgusting, and a half bottle of spoiled milk.

She sighed. "I've only been here since Friday, so I won't get discouraged," she told herself. "I came here 'cause I want to be a writer more than anything in this whole wide world. Nothing else matters."

Last November, Aunt Odessa, who was M'Dear's younger sister, had come to Smyrna for Thanksgiving. She'd encouraged Lilly Belle to apply for a place in the Harlem Young Writers Summer Workshop. "It's being sponsored by A'Lelia Walker," Aunt Odessa had explained. "She's the richest person in Harlem. A million-airess." Rich people impressed Aunt Odessa. She went on and on about how A'Lelia Walker had inherited her fortune from her mother, Madam C. J. Walker. "Honey, Madam Walker made loads of money from us colored women buying and selling her hair and skin products. She made us feel beautiful."

So Lilly Belle sent in ten poems she had written.

"Nothing ventured, nothing gained," Aunt Odessa had said. And she should know. She had moved to New York five years ago with little more than the clothes on her back. Now she was the manager of Sweet Lorraine's Dress Shop. "All the classy ladies shop there," Aunt Odessa had told Lilly Belle more than once.

Of course, Lilly Belle never dreamed there was a chance she'd be accepted to the program. But then a letter came addressed to Lilly Belle herself. She was one of eighteen students picked for the six-week program. As for the train tickets, A'Lelia Walker wrote that she would be pleased to provide train transportation. *Transportation*: Lilly Belle loved the sound of the word. So grown-up sounding.

Now here Lilly Belle was on 149th Street in Harlem, looking out a window at paved sidewalks, traffic lights, and street after street of brownstone buildings. The only bit of green was a tree here and there.

Suddenly, Lilly Belle opened her journal to a clean page. An idea for a poem was forming in her mind. She wrote:

A basket of biscuits
With butter and jam,
Two scrambled eggs
And a slice of ham,
Fresh fruit and milk
Help to round out the meal,
Then I open my eyes
And find none of it's real.

Chapter 2

First Friends

Aunt Odessa wasn't much of a housekeeper. And she didn't like to cook either. But she sure knew how to have a good time. And wherever she went, Aunt Odessa always looked stylish.

"Today we're going to have breakfast at a little pastry shop over on West 138th Street." To Lilly Belle that sounded so high-tone.

"Then after church we'll go over to the reception that A'Lelia Walker is hosting at the Dark Tower tearoom for you and the other summer students." Aunt Odessa made it all sound so wonderful. "Honey," she said, waving her hand, "the tearoom is the place to be seen these days." Aunt Odessa almost giggled, she was so excited.

Lilly Belle looked at the engraved invitation that had been sent to her. "The Dark Tower sounds like something out of a scary fairy tale," Lilly Belle said.

"No, girl. You just wait and see. She named it after a poem. The Walker beauty salon is there, too, right next door," Aunt Odessa said. "It's all very grand!"

"The tearoom is in her house?"

"Uh-huh! A'Lelia just opened it, because she wanted a place for famous artists, writers, and performers of all kinds to gather and share ideas. By invitation only," she added, fluttering her eyes.

"My, oh my," said Lilly Belle. She had a hundred more questions. But she thought she'd do what Aunt Odessa suggested: wait and see.

"And don't fret about what to wear," Aunt Odessa continued. "You'll be the most elegant girl there. Look what I picked for you." Aunt Odessa went to her closet and brought out the most gorgeous lavender dress from Sweet Lorraine's.

"For me?" Lilly Belle touched the dress to make sure it was real, then hurried into the bathroom to get ready.

Aunt Odessa's bathroom was nothing like the smelly outhouse back home. Lilly Belle flushed the toilet three times just to hear the gurgling swish of the water. The washstand wasn't a pitcher and bowl, but a sink set on top of a pedestal with handles marked hot and cold. No tin tub in here either. Instead there was a large bathtub, white and shiny as teeth. Its legs looked like the feet of a beast. Amazing.

Lilly Belle turned on the hot water and let it run. After her bath, she put on the beautiful lavender dress. It fit perfectly. It was hot and steamy in the bathroom, so she climbed up on the toilet seat to unlock and raise the window. A gust of cooler, dry air rushed in. She was still holding on to the sash when she heard someone shout.

"Don't jump. It can't be that bad. Please don't jump!"

Lilly Belle leaned out to see who was shouting.

A girl was at a window directly across the courtyard. She was waving her arms and calling, "Please, don't jump!"

"Me? Are you talking to me?" Lilly Belle called. "I wasn't thinking about jumping!"

The girl giggled. "I was just pretending this was a scene in a play," she said. "Howdy. My name is Cora Mae Jefferson. I'm going to be an actress one day . . . or maybe write plays."

"I'm Lilly Belle Turner. I want to be a poet. I'm here for the summer writing program at the Dark Tower."

"Well, I'll say! So am I," squealed Cora Mae. "I'm staying with my cousins Hazel and Thomas Edward Jefferson in apartment 601."

"Where are you from?" Lilly Belle asked.

"Little Rock, Arkansas. How 'bout yourself?"

"I'm from Smyrna, a little town outside of Nashville, Tennessee. I'm staying with my aunt Odessa. We're in 611."

"Glad to meet you," said Cora Mae. "I'd shake your hand if I could stretch that far." In the next breath she asked, "Do you like the city? I miss my mama and daddy something awful."

"I know what you mean. I've only been here two days, but I'm so homesick my stomach hurts. How long have you been here?" Lilly Belle asked.

"Come in on the train yesterday," Cora Mae said softly. "I aine never been 'way from home before. Talking about it makes me want to cry."

"New York is big and noisy," Lilly Belle said. "It makes my head spin. But I love writing. And we're going to be learning from the best. So I'm going to see it through."

"Oh, me, too. Me, three, four, and five!" Cora Mae added. "Think we could be friends?"

"We already are," said Lilly Belle. "We are first friends."

Chapter 3

A Russian

Although the church service began at eleven, Aunt Odessa was what she called "fashionably late." M'Dear would not have approved of being late for church just so people could get a good look at her outfit. M'Dear and Aunt Odessa were sisters, but to Lilly Belle they were as different as a rose was from a violet.

When church was over, they took a streetcar to West 136th Street. They walked past large, three-story mansions. They stopped in front of

108. "This is it," said Aunt Odessa, ringing the doorbell. "Don't be nervous," she whispered to Lilly Belle. "You are going to be just fine."

"I'm not nervous," Lilly Belle said. She tried not to fidget with the lace on the sleeve of her dress. Actually, Lilly Belle thought Aunt Odessa looked nervous. She kept fiddling with her hat, making sure it sat at the right angle on her head.

Suddenly, a tall, brown-skinned woman with bright almond-shaped eyes opened the door. She was wearing a silvery turban and a tiger-print silk tunic over a long black skirt. Her gold jewelry probably cost more than Daddy's wages for two years. Lilly Belle thought that A'Lelia Walker looked like a queen.

A'Lelia greeted them like old friends. "Come on in. Come in," she said in a big, welcoming voice. "I'm A'Lelia."

"This is my aunt Odessa and I'm Lilly Belle Turner. Pleased to meet you, Miss A'Lelia," Lilly Belle said, curtsying.

"Oh, drop the 'Miss,' honey. Just A'Lelia will do," she said matter-of-factly as she led them into the large parlor.

It was like being in a palace. Fresh flowers were everywhere. Furniture gleamed under the crystal chandelier. In the corner was the biggest piano Lilly Belle had ever seen. And there was a sky-blue Victrola for playing records. Lilly Belle didn't know colored people could live in such grandeur.

Aunt Odessa whispered to Lilly Belle, "Look over there. See that man? That's Countee Cullen, the poet you're always talking about."

Lilly Belle couldn't believe she was in the same room with her favorite writer. She had just read *Caroling Dusk*, his collection of poems

by young Negro writers. Then A'Lelia introduced Lilly Belle to a young woman who had on a hat with a feather in it. She was stylish, same as all the other guests. But Lilly Belle noticed the woman's expressive eyes.

"This is Zora Neale Hurston. She is a wonderful writer, and she will be your teacher for the summer," said A'Lelia.

Zora smiled. "Ah, so this is Lilly Belle Turner. I read the poems you sent," she said. "You have potential."

Lilly Belle tried not to blush as she thanked the woman. *Potential?* She knew that word. It meant beautiful things were inside her. It made her feel like a flower bud ready to bloom.

Next, A'Lelia took Lilly Belle's hand and took her over to meet the other student writers. Right away, Lilly Belle noticed a girl who was much taller than the other girls. But more than that, she was very pretty. Lilly Belle smiled at her, but the girl looked away.

A boy her age with round cheeks spoke first. "Hey. My name is Melvon. Melvon Parks. How do you do, Little Sheba?"

Lilly Belle looked at Melvon with a questioning look. "My name isn't Sheba."

"I know," he said. "That's what we cats call all the foxy girls."

"Do you like to use slang all the time?" she asked.

"Sure bet, Little Sheba!"

"Bet what?"

Melvon laughed. "How are you going to get along in Harlem if you don't know basic hep talk?" he said. "'Sure bet' means it is true or it's a winner."

Lilly Belle laughed, and so did he. There was something very likeable about Melvon. He told her he was from Atlanta, and that his father was a sociology professor at Atlanta University, the same as Dr. W. E. B. Du Bois had been. Melvon's mother was a dressmaker. He was staying with his oldest brother, Willie, who worked for *Crisis*, a famous colored magazine that Dr. Du Bois edited.

Melvon seemed so playful, it was difficult to imagine him ever having a serious thought. Lilly Belle wondered if she was a little bit too serious. Mama was always saying things like "Honey, don't worry about every little thing. You can't be perfect all the time."

Suddenly, Cora Mae came rushing over to the group. "Here y'all are," she said sweetly. "It's good to see you up close, Lilly Belle." She put her hand over her mouth to catch a giggle, but it was too late.

"Oh, no! Another Russian," the tall, older girl said with a bored sigh.

"Why no," said Cora Mae. Her eyes were wide and bright. "I'm not from Russia. I'm from Little Rock, Arkansas. My name is Cora Mae Jefferson. It's nice to meet y'all."

"Well, my name is Alice Gaylord. I was born right here in New York. In Harlem, Russians are what we call you Southerners who 'rush-in' to the city. Got it? *Rush-ins*. Russians run in with their country talk and country ways."

She pointed a finger dramatically at Cora Mae and Lilly Belle. "If I was you two, I'd drop the second name. Nobody uses Bea, Lee, Mae, and Belle, except . . ."

And Alice and a few of the older girls shouted together, "Russians!"

Chapter 4

---◦◦◦---

Standing in the
Presence of Greatness

Aunt Odessa was all business come Monday morning. It wasn't fashionable to be late for work. So she blew a kiss as she hurried out the door.

Aunt Odessa had written down the directions to the Dark Tower. Lilly Belle waited for Cora Mae to knock at the door. She was happy to have a friend, so they could find their way to the Dark Tower together.

On the short trolley ride, Cora Mae was very quiet.

---◈◈◈---

"What's the matter?" Lilly Belle asked. "Are you saving up all your words for class?"

"No. You can have New York. I don't like it. I don't belong here."

"You're just homesick. You'll get over it in a few days," Lilly Belle said.

"I am a rush-in, but all I want to do is rush back home."

"Is this all because of what that stuck-up girl Alice said? Pay no attention to her," said Lilly Belle. They hopped off the trolley at 136th Street. "Now come on or we'll be late."

When they reached the Dark Tower, Melvon was sitting on the front steps. "Hey, sweet peas," he said, smiling.

Cora Mae blushed. Lilly Belle rolled her eyes. "Hey, cool cat," she answered back.

Just then a fancy automobile pulled up. The driver rushed around to open the passenger door.

Alice stepped out. "Hello, country mice!" was all she said as she passed.

Melvon whispered, "She thinks she's cute because her father is Terrence Gaylord."

"Am I supposed to be impressed? I never heard of him," Cora Mae said.

"My brother told me that Alice's father owns buildings all over Harlem. And he's got big money! Alice thinks that makes her important."

"My stomach hurts," said Cora Mae.

"Come on. Don't be worried. It's going to be fine," Lilly Belle said.

In the parlor, the tinkling of a small bell brought the eighteen students to order. "Welcome once again to my tearoom," said A'Lelia. Zora Neale Hurston was beside her. "The real work begins today. I want to give artists a place where they can share and refine their work. You talented young people will be our writers of tomorrow. That is why you are here—to learn, to grow. To find your own voice, to develop its strength and see its power."

Melvon leaned over and whispered to Lilly Belle, "Whose voice would we use if not our own?"

Lilly Belle knew that A'Lelia didn't mean the voice they talked with. She was talking about their writing voice. A writer's voice was words on paper—the special way Lilly Belle used words made them *her* words, her *voice*, and nobody else's.

A'Lelia continued. "I believe I am standing in the presence of greatness. So, go about your work. Learn all you can."

As soon as A'Lelia left, Zora jumped right in. "Presence of greatness? Hmmph! I read yo' tiresome work," Zora began. "And frankly, I don't understand how any of you got in this program. Who tol' y'all you could write?"

Nobody dared answer. The room was silent. But Lilly Belle saw the twinkle in Zora's eyes and figured she might be like Grandma Turner, who sometimes said outrageous things just to make people sit up and listen.

Lilly Belle decided to speak up. "Were we *all* that awful bad?" she asked. "Don't some of us have potential?"

Alice groaned. "Lilly *Belle*, didn't anybody teach you that you don't say 'awful bad'? One or the other will do." Then Alice turned to Zora and explained. "She talks that way because she's from the South."

The girl next to Alice nodded.

"Oh, is that right? Well, it just so happens that I'm from the South myself. Did you know that?" Zora said. She never stopped smiling. "I'm from Eatonville, Florida," Zora continued. "Now that's *ree-aal* country."

Alice looked away and poked out her lips in a pout.

Zora never skipped a beat. "Where are you from, Lilly Belle?"

"Smyrna, Tennessee."

"Right outside Nashville? Been there. Good people. Good stories. I'm collecting folktales from down home, you know. And one day I'm going to put 'em all in a book."

Zora took off her hat and set it on the table. "So let's not waste any more time. Tell me about your favorite fruit."

"You mean write about it?" Alice asked, puzzled.

"What if you just don't like fruit?" someone asked.

"Then write about why you don't like fruit."
Zora paused. Her expression was serious. "Okay,
now," she said in a no-nonsense voice. "Chillen,
you're mine Monday through Friday, nine until
two. We've got a lot of hard work to do during that time. I hope you're ready for what's
ahead."

"Bring on the heat," said Melvon.

Chapter 5

A Piece of the Sun

The first week passed quickly. Cora Mae grew more and more homesick with every passing day. Alice made matters worse. She teased Cora Mae about her clothes, her hairstyle, even the way she sneezed.

"Alice's teasing doesn't seem to bother you," Cora Mae said to Lilly Belle before class.

"Oh, yes, it does," Lilly Belle answered. "I just don't let her see it. Alice picks on you because she knows it gets to you. Act like you don't care, and soon she'll leave you alone."

Then Zora entered the room, so Lilly Belle got out her notebook. Every day she wrote down every single word Zora said.

"There are no right or wrong words," Zora began. "Words are tools. The best words are the ones that express our thoughts and feelings. Ideas are everywhere. Write about what you care about most deeply. And rewrite, rewrite, rewrite. And then rewrite some more."

Then Zora read aloud a poem.

Gold and silver
I have none
But I'm not poor
For there is one
Who hugs me close
When day is done.

It was one of the poems Lilly Belle had sent in with her application. Part of her was proud because Zora was reading her work aloud. But another part of her feared how the other students might respond. Especially Alice.

Lilly Belle took a deep breath, blew it out slowly. Waiting.

"How does this poem make you feel?" Zora asked the class.

"Who wrote it?" Alice wanted to know.

"Doesn't matter," Zora answered. "I want to know how the words make you feel."

A few hands went up tentatively. Cora Mae began. "I think the poem means—"

Zora raised her hand to stop Cora Mae. "Forget about what it *means*. How does it make you *feel*?"

Cora Mae thought for a bit. "The words make me feel warm and comfortable—like being at home." She closed her eyes and hugged herself.

"The word *safe* comes to my mind," said

Melvon. "The hug is like a fence, keeping anything bad away."

"That's deep thinking," Zora told Melvon, appearing surprised.

"It makes me feel like I'm sitting with my face to the sun," said another student.

Lilly Belle smiled. They were getting all of that out of her poem? She remembered the day she read it to M'Dear, who cried happy tears. Zora was right—words were powerful tools.

A few more students made comments. Then Zora told the class that Lilly Belle was the author. "Now, tell us, what were *your* feelings when you wrote this?"

One look at Alice's smirking face and Lilly Belle was completely speechless. Finally, she said, "I-I-I don't remember how I felt."

That wasn't true. Lilly Belle remembered exactly how she felt. She just didn't want to say it in front of Alice and get teased later.

"Don't be ashamed to tell us," Alice said. She was smiling, but her words were laced with salt.

Remembering her advice to Cora Mae, Lilly Belle sat up taller in her chair. Then she said much louder than she meant to, "I wrote this poem to show M'Dear what's inside my heart!"

Alice made a face when she thought Zora wasn't looking. She whispered under her breath, "What kind of a countrified name is 'M'Dear'?"

Zora raised an eyebrow. "Your poem reminds me of my own mother," she said. "She always told me to jump for the sun. I worried how I could jump high enough to reach the sun. My mama's answer was, 'Jump as high as you can. At least you'll be up off the ground.' Good words spoken by a little countrified woman I lovingly called 'M'Dear.'"

It was very quiet, but Zora wasn't finished. "Lilly Belle, I can *feeeeel* the hug you wrote about. I hear your voice. Indeed I do."

Just then Alice didn't matter anymore. Lilly Belle felt like she'd just leaped up and grabbed a piece of the sun.

Chapter 6

Never Give Up

On Sunday night, Lilly Belle saw the light on in the bathroom of apartment 601. She hoisted herself up to the windowsill. "You there, Cora Mae?" she called out. The street sounds below were as loud as ever.

"Here I am," came the answer. Cora Mae's face popped up at the window. "Lilly Belle, don't be mad. . . . I-I-I'm going home. I'm leaving in the morning."

"Oh, no!" said Lilly Belle, although she wasn't surprised. "I'll miss you, girl."

"Me, two, three, and four," she said. "One day I'm going to read something written by Lilly Belle Turner. I will tell my children, 'I knew her.'"

"So Sweet Pea was too tender to take it," Melvon said before class started the next morning.

Alice overheard them. "One down and one country bumpkin to go," she said as she walked into the parlor for class.

"Not in your lifetime," Lilly Belle called back angrily. "I'm staying, and you just better get used to it."

After class, Melvon asked Lilly Belle to join him at a small restaurant on Seventh Avenue at West 141st called Logan's. "It smells good, looks clean, and the prices are right. Want to try it?"

Lilly Belle agreed.

At Logan's, Melvon ordered a cup of coffee

and a slice of cake. Lilly Belle never drank coffee at home. And she'd never had a store-bought dessert until breakfast at the pastry shop with Aunt Odessa. Mama made the best pies and cakes in three counties. Fact is, before coming to Harlem, Lilly Belle had only been to one restaurant in her life, Petunia's in Nashville.

There were a dozen wooden tables with mismatched chairs. Some of the older students from the Dark Tower were there. Melvon and Lilly Belle found seats near the window so they could watch the passersby.

"How does this place make you *feeeeeel*?" Melvon said. Lilly Belle laughed. It was a perfect imitation of Zora.

"I've never seen so many men dressed in suits and ties during the week," Lilly Belle said. "And women in hats. People back home only dress like that on Sundays or for funerals."

The coffee tasted bitter and the cake was dry, but Lilly Belle enjoyed being with Melvon. He was funny. They spent the afternoon in the café working on their assignment, which was to describe a bouquet of flowers.

"See each petal on the blooms. Smell them," said Melvon with Zora's flare.

"Stop playing," Lilly Belle ordered. "We have work to do. We can play later."

"Yes, ma'am," said Melvon. "Don't you ever let your hair down?"

"Not when there's work to do."

Their hard work paid off, though.

"Let me hear your voice, Mr. Parks," said Zora in class the next day.

"'Bouquet,'" he began, "by Melvon Parks."

To some, a store-bought bouquet of roses is lovely to give and to receive. Each flower is selected because it is the right color and matches all the others. The roses are then placed in an appropriate vase, each in its proper place among the other blooms. Perfection. A little too perfect for me.

I love a natural bouquet of flowers grown in an open field, randomly chosen and all different. There are no right or wrong colors. There are no flowers too tall or too small. A natural bouquet is wild and wonderful. Not perfect but better than perfect . . . beautiful.

Zora praised Melvon's work. "The world would be a little better off if we saw ourselves as a wild and wonderful natural bouquet," said Zora. "Nicely done."

Then turning to Alice, Zora said, "Let me hear from you."

"I-I don't have anything," Alice stammered.

She didn't offer any excuse and muttered an apology.

Zora looked at Alice. "Got stuck?" Before Alice could answer, Zora rushed on. "It happens to the best. So y'all are allowed an occasional attack of writer's block. But let's not make a habit of missing our work."

Later on at Logan's, Lilly Belle told Melvon, "Alice has had more than an 'occasional' attack of writer's block. And have you noticed she's never shared any of her writing in class?"

Melvon shrugged. "Maybe she thinks we're not smart enough to understand her voice," he said, teasing again.

But Lilly Belle was beginning to wonder about Alice.

Chapter 7

A Harlem Holiday

Every Saturday, Lilly Belle and Aunt Odessa went somewhere special in Harlem—to a play, a concert, a fashion show. Lilly Belle had been to the Savoy Ballroom on family night to see Bill "Bojangles" Robinson tap dance. After he performed, everybody got up to dance. Lilly Belle saw white people and black people dancing together on the same floor. Aunt Odessa also took her to hear James Weldon Johnson read from his book of poetry called *God's Trombones*. Now the Fourth of July weekend was coming, and A'Lelia and Zora had made special plans for the class.

The holiday began with the annual Fourth of July parade down Seventh Avenue in Harlem. Both sides of the street were packed with people—as many as in all of Smyrna.

A large marching band led the parade. Lilly Belle waved a small flag and cheered loudly. Women dressed in all white and men in blue suits and red ties walked proudly past.

"That's the Universal Negro Improvement Association," Aunt Odessa said over the noise. "They are followers of Marcus Garvey. I don't agree with everything Garvey preached, but I agree on some things. He wanted blacks to form their own businesses, start their own schools and banks, and even trade with African nations. Now that made sense to me."

Next came a group carrying a sign for the

Brotherhood of Sleeping Car Porters.

"They were the first colored workers to have their own union," said Aunt Odessa.

And after them came the veterans. Among the oldest men were a few who wore their Civil War uniforms. Everyone cheered for them loudly. But the crowd sent up a roar when the veterans from the Great War marched by. A woman dashed into the street and hugged a soldier who walked on crutches because he only had one leg.

Then tumbling clowns, trained dogs and horses, children's groups, and every organization in Harlem filed by, one after the other.

Lilly Belle had a wonderful time. And it wasn't over yet.

That evening, Zora took the students to see a motion picture show. None of them, not even Alice, had been to a motion picture before.

The movie was called *Body and Soul* and was about a wicked preacher and his brother. It starred the black actor Paul Robeson. He played the parts of both brothers. And the movie was directed by a black man, too. Oscar Micheaux. Watching pictures that moved! Lilly Belle couldn't get over it. It seemed like magic.

Afterwards Lilly Belle wrote a poem in her journal:

Pictures and words
Words and pictures
Pictures moving on screen
Showing a story
A wonderful show
Of pictures and words in motion.

The next day, A'Lelia held another July Fourth celebration at the Dark Tower.

Aunt Odessa bought Lilly Belle another dress from the shop. This one was peach-colored. It was very high style and the material felt luscious. Even Alice didn't have anything smart to say when Lilly Belle arrived.

She found her name at a place setting. Melvon rushed over to hold her chair. "Gosh, Lilly Belle, you look . . ." Melvon was lost for words. "Lovely." He sighed.

It was like being at a fairy-tale banquet.

Each place was set with china, crystal goblets, and silver. Last year on the Fourth, Lilly Belle's family had an outdoor barbecue, like always. At the Dark Tower there was no watermelon cooling in the tin tub. There was no chicken or ribs simmering on the pit. M'Dear wasn't fixing potato salad or deviling eggs.

Instead, Lilly Belle was dining on beef brisket, something called potatoes au gratin, green beans almondine, and hot buttered rolls. What Lilly Belle was enjoying in Harlem wasn't better. It was wonderful in a different way.

After the meal, a waiter brought out a dessert—a large cake decorated with roses that looked real. As Lilly Belle was finishing her cake, A'Lelia appeared and told her to come with her. "Some folks want to speak to you," she said. When they were in her office, she handed Lilly Belle the receiver.

Telephone? Lilly Belle had never used one before. Although there was a telephone at the corner store, people only used it in cases of death, birth, or other emergencies. A'Lelia had her very own right in her office. Was somebody in trouble at home, Lilly Belle wondered.

"Hello," she said.

"Baby girl," she heard her father say.

He sounded like he was right beside her.

"Daddy! Here I am," she said. "Is anything wrong?"

"No. We're all fine. And we're all here. Ms. A'Lelia arranged this call."

"Oh, Daddy, I miss you so much. Where's M'Dear?"

"Hello," M'Dear shouted as if trying to be heard all the way in New York. "Is that you, honey?"

"Yes, ma'am. It's so good to hear your voice," Lilly Belle said.

"Are you having a good time, learning how to write and all?" M'Dear asked. "We're so proud of you."

"Yes, ma'am. I write every day. My journal is almost full."

"That's good, baby. Real good!"

Lilly Belle felt her throat choking up when

she said, "Good-bye, Mama and Daddy. I love you!"

Later on, when Lilly Belle was back in Aunt Odessa's apartment, she sat at the kitchen table. She thought about Cora Mae back home in Arkansas with her family. Then she wrote:

> My stomach doesn't hurt.
> My head is not in pain.
> My throat doesn't scratch.
> I cannot complain.
> Yet I am sick—homesick.

Putting the words down didn't get rid of the ache. But they made her feel better.

Chapter 8

Word Pictures

Zora's assignments were never easy. After the holiday, everyone had to write an opening paragraph that would make the reader want to read more. "Paint a word picture so vivid, I can't wait to turn the page," said Zora.

The next day she chose Melvon to read his paper to the class:

I used to think all white people were rich. I never had been inside a white person's house who was not rich. Then one day I went to deliver a package to the Thompsons who lived down the road from us. They were white. There were no curtains at their window and no rugs on the floor. No bedding. No pretty little things sitting on the tables. The furniture was ragged and dirty. Abel Thompson was white, but he was poorer than us Negroes. I couldn't wait to tell my brother, who thought all white people were rich, too.

Zora praised Melvon for his creativity. "Well done, Melvon. You have made me want to read more. Do you like writing in the first person?"

Melvon nodded. "I like it because I am there, seeing and hearing everything that is going on in the story."

Zora's smile widened to a full grin. "I knew there was more to you than hep talk."

"That's such a Zora remark," Lilly Belle whispered.

Then, Zora called for Alice to read her paper. To Lilly Belle's surprise, Alice was eager and jumped right up. She cleared her throat, then began reading:

On my usual walk through the park, I saw a young woman—all alone on a park bench. It was the same bench where I often stopped to rest and feed the pigeons and squirrels. As I moved closer, I could see the woman's lips moving as if she was in a conversation with a phantom. She was a portrait of unhappiness. Her head drooped in despair. Her long, slender fingers fumbled with a small gold ring. What could have made her so sad? Who was she talking to? I wondered. Suddenly, the woman jerked off the ring and threw it as far as her strength would allow, and then she hurried away. Although the bench was empty now, I didn't want to sit down.

"That's crisp, fresh writing," said Zora. "Alice, I like how you used strong verbs like 'drooped' and 'fumbled.'"

"I like calling the woman 'a portrait of unhappiness,'" said Melvon.

Traitor! But as much as Lilly Belle hated to admit it, Alice had written a picture-perfect paragraph. Lilly Belle could see the young woman in her paragraph as clearly as she'd seen the moving pictures at the theater.

"Tell me, Alice," asked Zora, "did you experience this or imagine it?"

"I-I-I imagined it?" Alice's smile broke. "Isn't that all right? I thought you liked what I wrote?"

Zora raised an eyebrow. "I do. Very much. I simply asked because of the voice. It almost sounds as if you heard this story from an older person."

"Well. Yes. Yes." Alice was stuttering. "I remember now. I heard my grandmother tell about seeing a woman throw her ring away," she answered. "Some of what she told me must have stuck in my head," she added, a little more sure of herself.

"Ahh," said Zora. "The voice does sound grown-up, rather grandmotherly." She spent the rest of the class talking about voice again and praising Alice's writing.

If Lilly Belle had heard praise like that, her cheeks would have been sore from grinning. But Alice looked almost ashamed. She kept her head down, looking at her notebook the whole time. Alice was certainly a hard girl to figure out!

Chapter 9

Word Thief

Before Lilly Belle knew it, there were just two weeks left in the program. "I've almost gotten used to the nighttime city sounds," she told Aunt Odessa. "When I get back home, I probably won't be able to sleep—it'll be too quiet."

Aunt Odessa laughed. "Girl, I'm going to miss having you around here," she said.

"I'll miss you, too." Just the past weekend Aunt Odessa had taken Lilly Belle to the zoo. "M'Dear will never believe all the things I've seen here. Especially a real live tiger!"

Zora had also planned a trip. She was taking the class to visit the *Crisis* office. *The Crisis* was a magazine started by the National Association for the Advancement of Colored People—the NAACP. It contained essays, poems, and short stories, editorials, and features such as "The Horizon." This was a section about special events in the community. People who had done something outstanding were featured in the section called "Men of the Month."

"My father's picture was in the magazine," said Alice. "At home we have every issue that has ever been printed!"

Lilly Belle had never seen a black man's photograph in a magazine or newspaper. Harlem truly was an amazing place, she thought.

The *Crisis* office was small, so the class had to divide into two groups. Lilly Belle was so excited to meet the editor, Dr. W. E. B. Du

Bois, she couldn't speak. He was a famous educator and writer.

"We're going to have the privilege of publishing your final masterpieces," said Dr. Du Bois. His eyes twinkled when he smiled.

On a nearby work table lay stacks of old copies of *The Crisis*. Lilly Belle picked up one and turned to the table of contents. And to think she was going to see her name listed there alongside real authors.

"Put that down," Alice snapped. "You shouldn't be touching things!"

"Oh, that's all right," said Dr. Du Bois. "We put copies out for people to read. Take a few home with you, if you'd like."

So Lilly Belle did. Alice looked disgusted and walked away in a huff.

Later, at Logan's, Lilly Belle said to Melvon, "Did you see her try to grab that magazine out of my hands? Like I was a thief? She is the strangest girl I ever met!"

It wasn't until late that night that Lilly Belle started reading the copies of *Crisis*. She especially liked the section that featured first-time authors. She found a poem by Countee Cullen, and two stories by Zora. Zora Neale Hurston was a good writer, even as a beginner.

Then Lilly Belle's eye caught the title of a short story called "The Ring." It was by someone named J. Walker Reed. Lilly Belle read the first sentence.

On my usual walk through the park, I saw a girl I did not know.

Suddenly, she felt a shiver run up her spine. She continued to read.

She was sitting alone on a park bench where I often stopped to rest and feed the pigeons and squirrels. As I moved closer, I could see the woman's lips moving as if she was in a conversation with a phantom. She was a portrait of unhappiness. Her head drooped in despair.

Lilly Belle gasped. She couldn't believe it. But as she read more, there was only one way to explain what she saw right there on the page. Then she closed the magazine and sighed deeply. "No wonder Alice was acting so strange. . . . She was nervous," Lilly Belle whispered to herself. "She knew what she had done." Alice had copied almost word for word the opening paragraph of J. Walker Reed's short story and said it was hers. Alice was a thief—a word thief!

Chapter 10

The Confrontation

The next day, Lilly Belle waited in front of the Dark Tower for Alice to arrive. If only Cora Mae were here now! As soon as Alice stepped out of the car, Lilly Belle said, "We need to talk."

Alice tried to rush past her. "What about?" She waved to a man with gray hair in the car. "Bye, Daddy!" she said.

"I know what you did," was all Lilly Belle said. Then she held open the old issue of *The*

Crisis to J. Walker Reed's story. "You didn't think anybody would find out."

Alice was shaken. She blinked as if she might cry. "Are you going to tell?"

"I don't know yet." Lilly Belle was surprised to feel her own eyes fill with tears. "How could you do that?"

Alice gulped. "Ev-everybody copies out of books."

"Not everybody. And that's no excuse!" How many times had M'Dear said to Lilly Belle, "If everybody jumps off a bridge, are you going to jump, too?" Lilly Belle walked away, then she came back. "We've all been working hard. But all you've done is cheat! Cora Mae and I thought you were so much better than us. But you're not!"

Alice stomped her foot. Now she looked angry. "Who is J. Walker Reed anyway? Has anybody ever heard of him?"

Lilly Belle didn't back down, even though Alice was older and taller. "He was good enough to get published using his own words," she said. "What are you going to do for your final project? Steal somebody else's story? You have to tell Zora or . . ."

Alice sank down on the stoop. "Or you'll tell and I'll get put out! You don't understand. I can't get put out of this program. Look, I get a two-dollar allowance. You can have it all!"

"Don't insult me. I wouldn't take a penny from you!"

Alice's bottom lip began to quiver. She covered her face with her hands.

Lilly Belle wasn't moved by Alice's tears. "Cry all you want," she said. "You're still a word thief."

Alice sniffed. "I copied that story . . . because I-I was desperate."

Lilly Belle shook her head in disbelief. "Why?"

"Daddy will never forgive me if this gets out. If I do something that embarrasses him, th-that makes him look bad in public . . ." Alice's words trailed off. "It was his idea for me to be in this program," Alice explained. "He made me apply! So I took an essay from my brother's notebook. My father doesn't care if I want to be here or not."

"You don't want to be a writer?" Lilly Belle asked. Didn't everyone want to be one? Where would Lilly Belle be without her words? It would be like having no tongue.

"You are so good. Hearing your poems made me want to hand in something good, something everybody would like."

Lilly Belle was surprised to hear Alice talking this way. "How will you ever know how good you are if you don't find your own words?"

Alice sighed. "Look, if my father finds out about this, he'll probably send me away to school in New Orleans."

Lilly Belle didn't know if Alice was joking or not. She started up the steps.

"Are you going to tell Zora?" Alice asked once again.

"No, you are," Lilly Belle answered. Just then she decided something. "And if you want, maybe I can help."

"What? You'll help me, when I've been so hard on you?"

Lilly Belle waved her off. "Like you said, Alice. We *Russians* don't know any better."

Chapter 11

Fix It

Lilly Belle was there when Alice told Zora what she had done.

"It's called pla-gia-ri-sm!" Zora pronounced each part of the word.

"I am so sorry, and I promise I will never, ever, do it again. Please, *please*, just let me stay in the program."

Zora shook her head. It looked like it was all over for Alice. Then Zora turned to Lilly Belle. "Do you have something to say?"

Lilly Belle swallowed. "Yes, ma'am."

"Well . . ." Zora said, nodding her head.

"When I make a mistake at home," said Lilly Belle, "M'Dear always says, 'Fix it.' Zora, please, won't you give Alice a chance to make up for her mistake? I'd like to help."

Zora studied the two girls for what seemed like a long time. When at last she spoke, all she said was, "Okay, then fix it!"

That afternoon Lilly Belle made Alice go to Logan's.

"Why do you want to help her?" Melvon asked, right in front of Alice.

"Give her a chance," Lilly Belle said. "She's not so terrible once you see behind her false face."

"Wait a minute. Am I invisible here?" Alice said. "I may not be perfect, but I'm a person. Talk to me."

"I have nothing to say to you," Melvon said.

"Please, Melvon, as a favor to me?" Lilly Belle said.

Melvon stood with his arms folded. Finally he said, "Okay, Sheba. For you." But he didn't sound happy about it.

Zora's assignment for the next day was to write about a family member. "You write best about people and things you know," Zora had said. "Try to describe something about the person that you've felt but never said out loud before."

Now at Logan's, Lilly Belle closed her eyes. Instantly she saw her father sitting at the wooden table in the kitchen. His head was bent over a steaming cup of coffee. Then she began to write. After she'd finished, she shared it with Alice and Melvon.

He's a big man, bigger than most. He's a good man, better than most. He's a quiet man, still his booming voice can rattle the windows and shake a whole house. He only went through fourth grade. He can't read as well as me. I think it embarrasses him, but not me. He works so hard at the sawmill every day, yet he never seems too tired to hear about our day. No one gives more and expects less than the big, gentle man who is my daddy. He's the finest man I know.

"I don't know how you do it," Alice said, shaking her head. She bit the end of her pencil. "Our fathers are so different. He wants everything to be his way or no way at all."

"So? Write about that. Write what you just said," Melvon suggested.

Slowly, Alice began to write. Her head stayed bent over her notebook for a long time. When she was finished, Lilly Belle and Melvon asked to hear what she wrote. Alice licked her lips and started reading.

I live in a house where my father's voice out-shouts my mother's timid cries. He tells her what to wear, what to eat, what to believe, and what to do when, where, and why. Now his shouts are directed at me. But I hear Mama's whispers clearly. She says nobody can tell me what to think, what to feel, what to love.

Alice shrugged. "It's not too good."

"It sure lets me know what it feels like to live in your house," Melvon said.

"What's important is it's yours, Alice," said Lilly Belle. "Your words. Your very own voice."

In class the next day, Alice shared her work. When the class had finished discussing it, Zora looked at Lilly Belle and Alice and winked. "A'Lelia wants to see you both after class," Zora told them.

"What about?" Alice's eyes widened with fear. She shot a look at Lilly Belle, who shrugged her shoulders.

"I have no idea what A'Lelia wants," Zora said.

"Come with me," A'Lelia said. She led the girls down a hallway to the kitchen and down a flight of steps to the basement. A door opened and they stepped into the busy beauty parlor next to the Dark Tower.

"I would like to have a photograph of you both," A'Lelia said, "to promote our Walker hair and skin products."

Alice let out such a sigh of relief, it made

Lilly Belle laugh out loud. Then she said, "Do you mean like models?"

"You are beautiful young girls," A'Lelia continued, "who represent the best of our race—beauty and talent."

A'Lelia showed the girls around the shop. "I'd like to give each of you a complimentary hair wash, press, and curl before the photos are taken."

"Well, sure!" said Lilly Belle, and Alice nodded.

"I know you may be wondering what all of this has to do with being good writers," A'Lelia said. "You need a lot of confidence to write. And a little glamour never hurt any woman's self-confidence."

Chapter 12

A Song for Harlem

Melvon almost tripped over himself when Lilly Belle arrived at the Dark Tower with Aunt Odessa for the final program. "Your name is a flower and you look as pretty as one," Melvon said.

"What, no slang?" said Lilly Belle. She gave him a fake jab on his arm.

Lilly Belle remembered her first time at the Dark Tower. She had been so afraid then that she wouldn't make friends. She had been scared that her writing wouldn't be good enough. And she had been very frightened of Alice. Now there was a photograph in the parlor of Lilly Belle and Alice. A famous photographer named James Van Der Zee had taken it. Alice and Lilly Belle, their hair in curls, were smiling at each other in the photograph. And neither one of them was faking the smile.

Lilly Belle and Alice had become what Melvon called "thick." Lilly Belle liked the word "friends" better. She wished Cora Mae had stayed. She had missed out on so much.

The picture of Lilly Belle and Alice sat on an easel near the piano with a sign that said, "The New Walker Girls."

When Alice arrived, she said, "Daddy is going to love this, seeing his daughter's picture all over Harlem."

"Where is your father?" Lilly Belle asked.

"Oh! He has a very important meeting," she

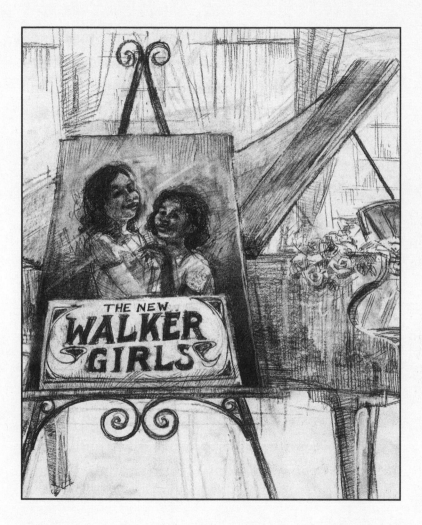

said quickly, pretending that it didn't matter.

Aunt Odessa was as beautiful as always. She sparkled like the chandelier over the piano in the Dark Tower. A'Lelia wore a royal-blue turban and large hoop earrings. Her dress was the same color trimmed in gold. She welcomed her guests to the closing program of the young writers workshop. She thanked Zora, who said a few words in praise of her students.

"I learned as much as I taught, and got as much as I gave. These are wonderful young people who are gifted and promising. I thank you, A'Lelia, for the opportunity. Now, I'm due for a long vacation."

Next A'Lelia introduced Melvon, who read his story. It was as funny and lighthearted as he was. "Our cat, Muffin, loves to bring my grandmother gifts," he began. "One day Muffin brought Granny a half-dead mouse and dropped it at her feet."

By the time Melvon finished his story about Muffin and Granny, everyone in the audience was laughing.

Some of the older students read their pieces. Then A'Lelia introduced Alice.

Alice stood. She looked around at the audience, stopping when her eyes locked on Lilly Belle's. Alice took a deep breath and began:

Once there was a princess who wanted to be accepted by the king. He was busy running his kingdom and didn't spend much time with his daughter. He wanted her to be special, though.

There was a great contest in the land. Who will write the best story? The princess tried writing her story, but nothing came to mind. She wasn't a very good writer. So she found an old book and copied a story written by someone else and put her name on it.

The day of the contest came. The princess was sure she would win. When it was her turn to read, she opened her paper. But something strange was happening. The words! They were disappearing. Right before her eyes, all the letters began to vanish. And whole lines of words began to fade off the paper. Soon all that was left was a blank piece of paper.

The princess thought nobody knew it. But a very wise woman saw what had happened. She knew the princess had stolen another writer's words. And the wise woman whispered to the princess, "To be a good writer, you must first be an honest writer."

When Alice finished, Lilly Belle jumped to her feet and clapped louder than anybody. She was so proud of Alice. Zora was beaming. "You fixed it just right."

Lilly Belle went last. Aunt Odessa kissed her for luck. Then she stood at the podium. Melvon winked. Zora smiled, and A'Lelia gave an approving nod.

"My poem is called 'A Song for Harlem,'" Lilly Belle told the audience.

A slow, long note
On a clarinet
Sliding through the opened window,
A stormy night
That leaves behind a morning rainbow,
A raised eyebrow, a quick nod,
A conversation
At the bathroom window,
Friends gathered at Logan's
To shuck and jive and jam
On words and ideas
That stretch the mind,

Hair, color, attitudes,
Friendships,
I will remember it all.
Good-bye, Harlem.
You are beautiful to me.
I will never forget you,
And I will sing your song forever.

Another Scrap of Time

"Look! Melvon's story is in *The Crisis* next to Lilly Belle's poem," Aggie said. "Whatever happened to him?"

Gee smiled. "Of all things, Melvon Parks became the owner of the largest black funeral home in Atlanta. Even so, Aunt Lilly Belle said he never lost his sense of humor."

"Did Lilly Belle's dream of being a writer come true?" Trey asked.

"She became a reporter in Pittsburgh, Pennsylvania." Gee took a newspaper from the trunk. "She worked at a newspaper called the *Pittsburgh Courier*, one of the oldest black newspapers in the country."

"Did she ever go back to Harlem?" Mattie Rae asked.

"Yes, but several years later, not until the 1930s." Gee became more serious. "It was the Great Depression. Harlem was a very different place. People had lost their jobs and their homes. Times were hard. They got even harder."

"What about Alice?" Aggie asked.

"Alice's father lost everything," Gee answered. "Mr. Gaylord moved his family to Los Angeles, California, where he hoped to get another start.

"When Alice got married in 1937, Lilly Belle went out to Los Angeles on the train to be her maid of honor."

"What about A'Lelia? Did she lose all her money, too?" Trey asked.

"No," said Gee. "A'Lelia didn't lose all her money. Though she had to close the Dark Tower."

Aggie wasn't listening. "Look what I found!" she said. She was holding a baseball with autographs.

"Josh Gibson, Cool Papa Bell, Satchel Paige. Oh, wow!" Trey took the ball.

"Who are they?" asked Mattie Rae.

"Only some of the greatest baseball players who ever lived!" Trey turned to his grandmother. "Where did this come from, Gee?"

"Lilly Belle's brother James gave her this autographed ball for her birthday. He played in the Negro Leagues."

"One of our relatives?" Trey was excited. "Tell us about him! Please! Please, with syrup all over it!"

"Okay, after lunch we'll come back up here. Then I'll tell you that story."

Harlem

————∞————

The Way It Used to Be

This is a fictional story, but it is based on a real period in our history known as "The Harlem Renaissance." After World War One, many African Americans left the segregated South and moved north, hoping for a better life. During the 1920s, Harlem, a neighborhood in New York City, seemed to offer it all—freedom, opportunity, and jobs. It was especially the place to be for writers, poets, and musicians. They were free to express themselves in new and wonderful ways. And they did, creating extraordinary works that we still enjoy today. Harlem was the center of the artistic explosion of the black experience in America. Some people called Harlem "the Black Capital of the country."

This is the way it used to be in Harlem during the 1920s.

✦ 1919: There were race riots throughout the country. So many blacks were murdered, it was called "Red Summer."

✦ 1919: Madam C. J. Walker died at the age of fifty-one. She left her hair and skin care company to her daughter, A'Lelia Walker Robinson.

✦ 1920: James Weldon Johnson, a lawyer and very famous writer, became executive secretary of the National Association for the

Advancement of Colored People (NAACP).

✦ 1921: Langston Hughes's first poem, "The Negro Speaks of Rivers," was published in the June issue of *The Crisis*. He was nineteen years old.

✦ 1923: Jean Toomer's famous book *Cane* was published to rave reviews.

✦ 1923: The Department of Labor reported that 500,000 blacks had left the South. A record number of them migrated to Harlem.

✦ 1925: *The New Negro*, the first anthology of Harlem Renaissance writers, was published. Alain Locke was the editor. Besides Locke, W. E. B. Du Bois, Jessie Fauset, and Charles Johnson were leading voices in the literary scene.

✦ 1925: Oscar Micheaux, a black filmmaker, produced *Body and Soul*, starring Paul Robeson in his first film appearance.

✦ 1925: Louis Armstrong's first recordings with his Hot Five gave jazz a new sound.

✦ 1926: The Paul Laurence Dunbar Apartments, a 511-unit complex, were completed. It was the first large co-op for blacks and named for the famous poet.

✦ 1926: Famous poet Countee Cullen earned a masters degree from Harvard and became assistant editor at *Opportunity: A Journal of Negro Life*, a publication of the National Urban League. He wrote a literary column called "The Dark Tower." A'Lelia Walker borrowed the name for her salon. Later the award-winning poet would become an eighth-grade English teacher.

✦ 1927: Duke Ellington and his band opened at the famous Cotton Club in Harlem.

✦ 1928: A'Lelia Walker opened the Dark Tower in her home at 108 West 136th Street. It was a place where writers and artists gathered to eat and discuss the arts. She encouraged local youth to participate in some of the activities at the Tower. Before the year was over, however, A'Lelia closed the salon. She died on August 16, 1931, of high blood pressure.

✦ 1928: Zora Neale Hurston graduated from Barnard College, which she attended on scholarship. She also taught to cover her expenses. Later she attended graduate school at Columbia Universtiy. Her most famous novel, *Their Eyes Were Watching God*, would be published in 1937.

✦ 1929: The stock market crashed, bringing about the Great Depression of the 1930s. It was the beginning of the end of the Harlem Renaissance.

Harlem Organizations

National Association for the Advancement of Colored People (NAACP)—organized in 1909 by blacks and whites. W. E. B. Du Bois was one of the founders and the first editor of *The Crisis*. The purpose then, as it is now, was to address the issues of equal rights and protection under the law for all citizens as guaranteed by the U.S. Constitution.

Brotherhood of Sleeping Car Porters—the first black union, organized by A. Philip Randolph on August 25, 1925, at the Elks Hall in Harlem. The purpose was to help bring humane working conditions for porters who worked for the Pullman

Sleeping Car company. The Pullman Company didn't recognize the union until October 1937.

National Urban League—originally organized in October 1911 to help poor Southern blacks make the transition from farm life to city life.

Universal Negro Improvement Association—organized by Marcus Garvey to instill pride in the black race, build trade among people of color around the world, and help to make black people more independent. Believing that blacks would never get a fair chance in a white-dominated society, Garvey began his "back-to-Africa movement," which inspired a lot of followers. He was tried and convicted unfairly of fraud in 1924 and made to leave the country. The organization Garvey started continued and later became the foundation for other black self-help groups.

TURN THE PAGE FOR A LOOK AT
THIS FAMILY'S STORY
FROM 1937—

In Gee's Attic

There was always something new for the cousins to discover in their grandmother's attic. Well, "new" wasn't the right word. There was always something old to discover—things that had belonged to different people in their family, most of whom had lived long before Trey, Aggie, or Mattie Rae was born.

Earlier, Gee had told them about Aunt Lilly Belle Turner, who had gone to New York to study writing. Now Trey wanted to hear all about a baseball that had belonged to Lilly Belle's brothers.

"Everybody always called the Turner brothers by their nicknames, Tank and Jimbo," Gee

explained. "All except Lilly Belle. To her they were always Peter and James."

"Who gave them this ball?" Mattie Rae asked.

"Josh Gibson. He was the slugger on the Homestead Grays," Gee answered. "See his autograph? There are other ones, too."

Trey took the ball from Mattie Rae. "Satchel Paige signed this! He was a great pitcher," he said. "He's in the Baseball Hall of Fame."

"Tank and Jimbo knew players in the Hall of Fame?" Aggie was impressed.

"Tell us more about Tank and Jimbo," Trey asked.

Mattie Rae was still trying to get the baseball back from Trey, until Gee handed her an old photo from the trunk.

Gee sat on a stool and began her story. "This is a picture of the Homestead Grays."

"You mean there were teams with just black players?" Mattie Rae said.

"Oh, yes. None of the major-league teams would let blacks play. And back in 1937 when this photo was taken, the Homestead Grays were as good as any major-league team around—or better."

Chapter 1

------◦◦◦◦◦------

Caught!

James and Peter Turner looked like twins, even though James was a full year older than Peter. Now, with their sister Lilly Belle working at a Pittsburgh newspaper, there wasn't anybody in Nashville, Tennessee, who called the boys by their real names. James was Jimbo and Peter was Tank. They did everything together, and what they loved best was playing baseball. If only they had a team to play on . . . and other teams to play against.

They hardly ever got to watch games either.

But then Tank found a way to sneak into the Sulphur Springs Ballpark to see the Negro Leagues games. For free! It was risky, though.

Big, bad Joe Munday was the ballpark manager.

"I know you squirrels are sneakin' and peekin' but I'll catch you one of these days," Mr. Munday had told the brothers many times. "And when I do, I'm gonna call the police!"

"But we're just kids," said Tank, who was eleven.

"Old enough to go to the Tennessee State chain gang." Then Mr. Munday lowered his voice. "You'll be crackin' rocks from sunup till sundown for the rest of your lives."

Still Tank decided that watching a good baseball game was worth the risk. See, Tank loved taking chances. Like when Sammy Franklin double-dared Tank to ride down Deacon Hill freehanded on his bicycle. It was crazy, but Tank did it. Of course, he fell and broke his nose. But when Sammy called Tank a fool, it was Jimbo who tried to break Sammy's nose.

Tank always counted on his brother to have his back. So he went on his merry way, getting into hot water and expecting Jimbo to fish him out. And that's why Jimbo followed Tank whenever he sneaked into the ballpark.

It was a hot day in June. The Homestead Grays were playing the Tennessee All-Stars in a five game series, over the next eight days.

Same as always, Tank pushed aside the loose board in the fence behind the center-field bleachers. The opening was just large enough for him and Jimbo to squeeze through. Then they crawled on their bellies under the bleachers until they found a perfect spot to watch the game.

The boys were especially excited today, because

the Grays had one of the greatest new players. Josh Gibson had just joined the team. Tank already knew about him. He read everything he could on the Negro League players. Josh was a home-run threat every time he came to bat. Ordinarily Tank and Jimbo rooted for the Tennessee team, but the Grays were special. With Josh Gibson, they could make the 1937 season one of the best ever in the National Negro Baseball League!

The umpire yelled, "Batter up!"

Tank watched Josh Gibson take long strides to home plate. He was a muscular man with powerful arms and a big smile. He set his bat. The All-Star pitcher, Lee Webb, hurled two balls and then a blazing fastball strike.

"Look at him," Tank shouted. "Gibson is holding the bat with one hand now."

"Yeah, just like Babe Ruth!" said Jimbo. "He's mocking the pitcher."

Gibson pointed to right field.

"Look! He's showing where he's going to hit a homer!" said Jimbo.

"Do you think Gibson is as good as the Babe?" Tank asked.

"I think so," Jimbo said. "But there's no way to tell, 'cause coloreds can't play in the majors."

"One day they will," said Tank.

"When pigs fly, maybe," Jimbo put in.

The pitcher was in the windup when suddenly, Tank felt two strong hands grab his feet and pull him backward.

"Run, Jimbo," shouted Tank. "Munday's got me!"

Jimbo crawled away on all fours and managed to escape.

"Ha! Finally got one of you squirrels," Mr. Munday said, and laughed. It sounded wicked.

Tank spit out dirt and coughed. Mr. Munday

dragged him to his feet. "Please, sir, don't put me on the chain gang. It would break my mother's heart," he pleaded.

All at once the crowd sent up a roar. Cheers and shouts hung on the muggy June air. Josh Gibson had hit a home run with one hand!

Munday cupped one hand over his eyes to follow the ball. "Look at it fly," he said, and then whistled through his teeth. For a brief moment he loosened his grip on Tank.

Tank twisted out of Munday's hold and dashed away.

"If I ever see you around this park again, you're gonna get it! Hear me?" Munday called after him, and shook his fist.

Tank never answered—never looked back or stopped running.